Tasmanian Terror

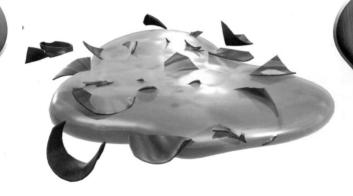

Anthony McGowan
Illustrated by Jon Stuart

From:	STING, Charles
To:	Top secret

Subject: TEAM X

To *******

Following the arrest of Dr X, we have made several changes at NICE.

- NICE is now the *National Institute for the Conservation of Earth.*
- Dani Day has been appointed to the position of Senior Scientist.
- The mission of NICE is to help protect the planet and the precious things in it.

In order to help NICE in its mission, Dani Day has employed a team of four agents. She assures me that they are highly capable. In order to protect the agents, their real identities must remain a secret. They have been given the name Team X. Their operation status is now **code green**.

I will keep you informed of any further changes.

Regards

Charles I. Sting
**Director of Operations,
NICE**

Important
Agent Information
Read this first

The TASMANIAN

SLIME FEST!

Picnickers got more than they bargained for yesterday in York Plains park. The park's picnic area was covered in thick, green slime, which trapped a family who were having their lunch. No one is thought to have been hurt.

Early yesterday morning, local man, Danny Reardon, reported to police that a number of large rocks had appeared overnight in the park.

Mr Reardon said, "I go jogging in this park every morning. I always take the same route so I couldn't believe it when I saw the huge rocks in my path. They were covered in a strange pattern."

When the police arrived at the scene, there was no sign of the rocks. The picnic area has now been cordoned off. Police have appealed for any further witnesses to come forward as they investigate the mysterious events.

TEAM X DESTINATION: TASMANIA

Continent: Australasia
Country: Australia
Destination: Tasmania
Climate: Variable and changeable. On the west coast, the average rainfall is around three metres a year. On the east coast, average rainfall is less than 20 centimetres.

Tasmania is Australia's only island state. It is situated off the south-east coast of Australia and is separated from Australia by a stretch of water known as the Bass Strait. The island covers an area of 68000 square kilometres. It contains animals and plants only found in Australia.

Chapter 1 – The falling star

Location: The Unwin's Farm, Tasmania

Mr Unwin looked out of his window at his dry fields. He ran a sheep farm in Tasmania, and there had been no good rain for two years. The little river that ran through his land was now no more than a muddy trickle. The grass was brown, and the leaves in the trees crackled in the faint breeze.

"Not a cloud in the sky," he said, glumly to his wife, Mary.

She joined him at the window.

"If this goes on, Jim ..." she said.

She didn't have to finish the sentence. Mr Unwin knew what she was going to say. They would have to sell the farm.

The thought made him desperately sad. The farm had belonged to his great-grandfather. The family had always looked after the land carefully and tried to encourage the local wildlife. There were duck-billed platypuses in the river and spiny echidnas in the woods.

The platypuses and echidnas were special because they were the only mammals in the world that laid eggs.

There were also Tasmanian devils nearby. These scavengers have a fierce snarl and a high-pitched scream. Most other sheep farmers would have tried to get rid of them, but the Unwins believed that the native animals of Tasmania had the right to live in their own land. Mr Unwin's father had told him about the Tasmanian tiger, a stripy marsupial wolf that had died out long ago. Mr Unwin hoped that there might still be a few living somewhere in the wilds, perhaps even on his own farm.

What most worried Mr Unwin was that, if he sold the farm, the new owner might cut down the beautiful trees and drive away the animals.

Tasmanian animals

Platypus

- The platypus lives in streams, rivers and lakes.
- It has a sensitive, flexible bill, which it uses to find food and navigate in murky water.
- It has large, webbed front feet and a broad, flat tail, which helps it swim.

Echidna

- The echidna (or spiny anteater) is covered with coarse hair and short, pointy spines. When threatened, it rolls into a prickly ball for protection.

- It eats ants and termites which it pulls in with its long, sticky tongue.
- Like the platypus, echidnas lay eggs instead of giving birth to their young.

Tasmanian devil

- The Tasmanian devil is a scavenger.
- It lets off a strong, unpleasant smell when threatened.
- It makes loud, high-pitched screeches and howls.
- The Tasmanian devil hunts at night. Its long whiskers help it to feel in the dark.

Tasmanian tiger [thought to be extinct]

- The Tasmanian tiger looked like a dog with brown fur and black stripes across its back.
- It was hunted to extinction in the early 1900s.
- The last known tiger died in 1936.

At that moment, Mary and Jim noticed a streak of light in the sky. It only lasted for a couple of seconds, and then there was an explosion. The ground trembled, and the windows shook in their frames.

"What on earth was that?" said Mary.

"I'm going to find out," Jim replied, and reached for his hat.

Chapter 2 – The mission

Max, Cat, Ant and Tiger had been called to the headquarters of NICE.

"Listen up, everyone," said Dani Day, the senior scientist at NICE. "I've got a mission for you."

"Great," said Tiger. "Where are we going this time? I hope it's the jungle, and we've got to rescue a giant anaconda from some poachers or something cool like that."

"Well," said Dani, "it's not quite the jungle. We've had a report of some unusual rocks ..."

"Rocks? You've got to be kidding!"

"If you'll let me finish, Tiger ..."

"Sorry."

"Something strange has been happening in a small town in Tasmania, which is an island off the south-east coast of Australia. A local man told the police that a number of large rocks had mysteriously appeared overnight in a park. The police didn't give it high priority ..."

"Not that surprising," Tiger said sarcastically.

Dani ignored him. "When the police finally did arrive the rocks had simply disappeared."

"Rocks that aren't there?" said Cat. "Doesn't sound like much of a mission to me."

"But that's not all," said Dani. "The local newspaper also had a story about some picnickers who had become trapped in thick streams of green slime."

"Slime – that's a bit more like it!" Tiger jumped up.

"And you think these two things are linked?" asked Max.

"That's for you guys to find out."

Not long later, a blue light shimmered in a patch of bushes in a park in the east of Tasmania. One by one the children jumped out of the X-gate. The X-gate teleport allowed the children to get anywhere in the world in seconds.

"That thing really messes with my hair," said Tiger.

"You can worry about your hair later," said Max. "After we've found out what's going on. Let's fan out. Keep your eyes peeled for unusual rocks or trails of slime."

Chapter 3 – On the slime trail

Team X spread out in a line, searching for anything unusual. It was early in the morning and there weren't many other people about.

"What is that?" yelled Cat after a few minutes.

"It's a kangaroo," said Tiger, "obviously."

"Actually, it's a wallaby," replied Ant. "You can tell, because it's smaller."

"It's cute ..." said Cat, "... arrgggghhhh!"

Distracted by the wallaby, Cat had stepped right into a thick trail of gooey slime. It looked like green hair gel, but it smelled of rotten cabbage. Losing her footing, Cat slipped over and began to slide in the slime down a nearby slope.

"HELP!" she screeched, as she slid away from the others.

Ant grabbed her arm, but she dragged him over. With a horrible squelching sound, they both careered down the slope, landing in the foul green mess at the bottom.

Tiger carefully peered over the edge of the slope. "I think we can safely say that we've found the slime trail."

"Are you OK?" called Max.

Ant groaned.

"Yes," Cat replied eventually, "we're fine."

"Right, so now we follow the trail," said Max.

"But which way?" said Tiger. The trail went down the steep slope in front of them and also off to the left, down a much more gradual slope.

"Looks like we have to split up. Tiger, you come with me so I can keep an eye on you. Cat and Ant, you've already made a head start on your trail!"

Chapter 4 – Cat and Ant's discovery

Once they had freed themselves from the slime, Cat and Ant began to jog along by the side of the slime trail.

"Have you noticed the bushes?" said Ant.

"What about them?"

"Lots of them seem to have been stripped of their leaves."

"Yes, and look over there," Cat said, pointing at a patch of bare ground with a few scattered stalks. "Looks like the flowers have gone, too."

After a while, the slime trail led them into a little valley. The trees closed in overhead, blocking out the sun. It was suddenly very quiet, and they felt rather alone.

"It's a bit creepy in here," said Ant, looking nervously around. He knew all about the fierce reputation of the Tasmanian devil. "I wonder if Max and Tiger have found anything."

"I don't know, but I've certainly found something … and I don't like it."

Ant came over to see what she had discovered.

The slime trail led to an open patch of ground. It looked as though there had been an explosion of some kind, as the trees and bushes around the clearing were bent and broken backwards. There was slime everywhere, hanging from branches and dripping from leaves. And not just slime; there were big, broken pieces of what looked like stone or pottery scattered around the clearing.

"What the ..." Ant just stood there with his mouth open.

"Snap out of it, Ant," Cat said, urgently. "Help me collect some of these things, whatever they are. We can send them back through the X-gate to Dani. She might be able to analyse them."

Ant picked up one of the strange flat pieces of pottery.

"There's something familiar about the design on this," he mused to himself. "I've seen it before somewhere, I know I have."

"What was that?" Cat said with alarm.

"What?"

"That rustling sound."

"I didn't hear anything."

"Look!" Cat's mouth fell open and she stared behind Ant.

Ant was still studying the pottery.

"Yes, it's very peculiar …"

"No, no! Ant!"

"In fact, I wonder if it is pottery at all?" Ant frowned at Cat who was gesturing behind him. He glanced over his shoulder and his mouth fell open, too.

Through the trees, they could make out a huge round object. A wet, squelching sound grew louder as the object approached them.

"A snail!" shouted Ant.

But this snail was gigantic – twice the height of either of them. The massive shell was covered in a pattern – the same design as was on the pieces of pottery. As it approached, it gorged on bushes and branches in its path.

"RUN!"

Chapter 5 – The lake of mystery

Max and Tiger followed the slime trail through the park and out into the countryside. Eventually they came to the ridge of a hill where a wire fence had been knocked flat.

"Looks like whatever made that slime trail was big enough to bash down this fence," said Max. "We'd better be careful."

He signalled Tiger to keep down. Together they peered over the top of the ridge. Below them, they saw green fields, a small lake and some farm buildings.

"Wow," said Tiger. "I thought there was a drought here?"

"Well, this farm obviously has water. It must be fed from an aquifer."

"A whatquifer?"

"Aquifer. It means there's a layer of rock underground that traps water. But my guess is that the lake has something to do with this mystery. Can you see how the slime trail leads down to it?"

"Yes, I see. Or rather it leads *from* it. Do you think some kind of monster came out of the lake? And have you noticed that there aren't any animals in the fields, eating all that nice green grass?"

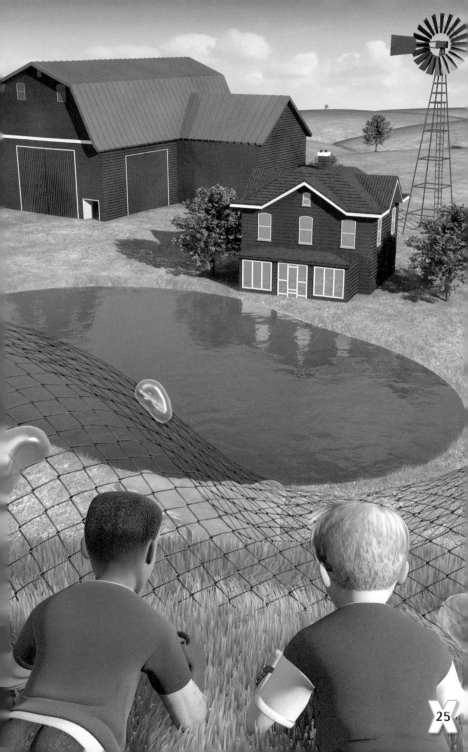

Max and Tiger exchanged worried glances.

"Perhaps they're all in that big barn over there?" Max suggested. "I think I see the farmer heading towards it."

At that moment, they heard the sound of people approaching. It was Cat and Ant and they were looking spooked.

"Did you find anything?" asked Max.

Cat and Ant looked at each other.

"You could say that," Ant replied.

Chapter 6 – Pulling the wool over their eyes

Cat quickly explained about the strange pottery fragments.

"So what were they, then?" Max enquired.

"Snails."

"WHAT?"

Ant told them about the gigantic snail. Then he explained how he and Cat had outrun it, and then used Cat's watch to track Max and Tiger.

"We sent a fragment of the shell to Dani. The DNA analysis was quite clear. The pottery *was* pieces of a giant snail shell. And there were low-level traces of a weird new type of radioactivity."

"It gets worse, though," chipped in Cat. "The thing is, that we think the snails, well, err ... exploded."

"You're kidding."

"I wish we were," replied Ant. "My theory is that something – probably this new type of radioactivity – made these perfectly normal snails grow to giant size, but in the end their bodies couldn't take it and ..."

"Splat!" said Tiger.

"Exactly."

"Well, whatever happened, it all began here,"
said Max. "Cat, can you use your watch to see
what's happening in that barn down there?"

Cat flicked up the magnifying attachment,
and they all gathered round to look. They saw a
tall farmer carrying bales of hay into the barn.

"You were right, Max," said Tiger. "He *has* got the animals in there."

Then the farmer disappeared for a couple of minutes. When he came back, he was carrying a huge electric hedge trimmer.

"He must be going to trim the hedge," said Cat.

"What hedge?" said Ant. "He's taking it into the barn!"

"Right," said Max, decisively. "It's time we found out just what's going on here. "Let's get down there and have a closer look."

Trying hard to stay out of sight, the children ran down to the barn. They had to pass the lake on the way.

"Is it my imagination or is that lake glowing, ever so slightly?" mused Cat.

"I think you're right," said Max. "We'll check it out after we've had a look in the barn. First, we need to shrink so we aren't spotted."

Team X turned the dials on their special watches anticlockwise. A bright blue X appeared in the centre of each one. They pushed the X and, in an instant, the team were micro-sized.

"Now, let's find out what's going on inside the barn."

The barn had two entrances. There was a big door, through which the farmer had gone, and a smaller door at the side, slightly ajar. The children sneaked quietly up to the side door and looked in.

What they saw amazed them.

Towering over them was a sheep that was bigger than an elephant. Beside it, standing on a step-ladder, the farmer was using the hedge trimmer to shear wool from its side. The sheep hardly seemed to notice. There were many more giant sheep in the barn, some shorn, others still encased in their thick coats of wool.

In a few minutes, the job was done. The farmer, Mr Unwin, put the wool in a trailer attached to the back of a tractor and drove out of the barn.

"This is getting really weird," said Tiger. "First giant snails and now giant sheep!"

"I think we need a closer look at those sheep," said Max. "Let's grow back to normal size. Tiger, you keep an eye on the door – tell us if the farmer comes back."

The children pushed the X on their watches, and soon they were full-sized again. They edged towards the nearest sheep.

"Do you think they're dangerous?" asked Cat.

"I doubt it," replied Ant. "Sheep are very placid animals." He reached up to stroke the sheep's soft wool. "Obviously the same thing that made the snails grow has affected the sheep."

"Oh, no," groaned Cat. "Does that mean that the same thing will happen to them?"

Before anyone had the chance to answer, Team X heard a gruff voice behind them.

"And who are *you*? This is private property. I'll have the police on you!"

The children span round to see the tall farmer approaching, with Tiger skulking along in front.

Chapter 7 – The explanation

"Somehow," said Max, coolly, "I don't think you'll be going to the police. You might find it hard to explain away these." He pointed with his thumb towards the monster sheep.

"Yes, well, err ..." stammered Mr Unwin.

"We need to talk," Max continued. "There are some facts we both need to know."

Just then, Mrs Unwin appeared at the barn door.

"Let's have a cup of tea and talk this all through," she said, in a kindly voice. "Anyone like a slice of cake?"

Over tea and cake, Mr and Mrs Unwin explained what had been going on at their farm. When Mr Unwin went to investigate the big bang, he found a smouldering hole.

"I reckoned a meteorite had hit," he said. "Went straight down into the ground."

"Shortly afterwards, the hole had begun to fill up with water," chipped in Mrs Unwin.

"Just as I suspected," nodded Max, "the meteorite must have reached the aquifer."

"Dead right, mate," said Mr Unwin. "And that was good news. We needed water. The place was as dry as a bone."

But the Unwin's good luck did not stop there. The animals that drank from the new lake began to grow at an astounding rate.

"Soon each sheep was producing more wool than a whole herd. It meant I could afford to invest in the land, making sure the environment was properly preserved for native animals."

"That's all fine in principle," said Ant. "But do you understand the terrible consequences if any of the local wildlife drank this water? You'd have Tasmanian devils bigger than lorries ..."

"I'm not daft," said Mr Unwin. "That's why I put a strong fence all round the lake."

"Would that be the same fence we saw knocked down, up beyond that hill?" asked Max.

"Down? Are you serious? I'd better get up there and fix it."

"But that's not all," said Cat. "The fence was knocked down by some giant snails. We followed their trail. At the end of it all we found were bits of splattered snail."

"What ...?"

"It's unstable," said Ant. "No animal can take that much growth in such a short time. The snails just, well, exploded."

"And so what about my sheep?" The colour drained from Mr Unwin's face.

"It's hard to know exactly, as snails are molluscs and sheep are mammals. It may be that they react differently," explained Ant.

"But they might react the same?"

"It's possible."

"Can I ask you something, Mr Unwin," said Cat. "Have you always been that tall?"

"I thought you seemed bigger recently," said Mrs Unwin. "You haven't been drinking the lake water, have you?"

"Well, maybe just a mouthful – I didn't want the animals to drink it if it was dangerous, so I sort of tested it ..."

"You're very lucky we came," said Max. "I can't explain everything, because it's top secret, but I can say we're not here by accident. And we can help."

"Can you put my sheep back the way they were? I'd be heartbroken if they went and blew up, like those poor old snails."

Max conferred with the others.

"I think," said Ant, "that if we use the combined power of our watches, we can shrink them."

"Let's give it a go," said Max.

Chapter 8 – Shrinking sheep

Max stood beside the first giant sheep. Tiger stood next to him. Cat and Ant joined them. Max nodded, and together they aimed their watches at the sheep and turned the dials twice to the left. A bright green X appeared in the centre of each watch and four thin arcs of green light shot towards the startled sheep. A second later, it was normal-sized again.

Within a few minutes, the whole herd was back to normal. Tiger went to get Mr Unwin.

"Makes the barn look huge," Mr Unwin said ruefully.

"Better than having chunks of exploded sheep splattered all over the place," said Tiger.

"Tiger, you're sick," said Cat.

Tiger chuckled.

"And now it's your turn," said Max to Mr Unwin. "We can't show you how we'll shrink you. Will you trust us?"

Mr Unwin nodded.

"I'm going to ask you to turn around, Mr Unwin."

He did as Max asked and Team X gave him a quick blast.

"The next question," said Max, when they had finished, "is what to do about the lake – we can't just leave it contaminated. Anything that drinks the water is going to grow then blow."

"I've been thinking about that problem," said Ant. "Because the radiation is at quite low levels, it shouldn't take too long to decontaminate itself if we can get rid of the source."

"You mean the meteorite that Mr Unwin saw?" asked Max.

"Precisely."

"But how will we reach it?" said Cat. "It must be buried under the lake."

"Well," said Max, "the meteorite is probably buried in the rock beneath the lake."

"Can we use the Driller?" said Cat, enthusiastically. The Driller was Team X's underground X-craft, designed by Dani Day. Its nose ended in a sharp spiral drill that was designed to cut through any material, and its solid mechanical claws could penetrate the hardest earth.

Not long later, a micro-sized Max and Cat were sitting in the sturdy metal Driller. Dani had sent it through the X-gate. They were going to dig down at an angle through the ground, until they reached the meteorite.

The Driller's path

Dani had fitted the Driller with a Geiger counter, so it could home in on the meteorite. The plan was to use Max and Cat's watches to shrink the meteorite down, and then put it in a special lead-lined canister Dani had designed.

The nose began to spin, and the metal claws cut into the ground, and in a few seconds the Driller had disappeared beneath the earth.

Chapter 9 – Tasmanian devil

Back in the kitchen, Mr Unwin told Tiger and Ant all about the farm and the drought, and how the giant sheep had looked like the solution to all his problems.

"But once the water has been decontaminated you'll be able to use it safely," said Ant. "The aquifer will still be there, and the water will still flow into the lake."

"I hadn't thought of that," said Mr Unwin, brightly. "With the water, we'll be able to grow more crops, and the grass will be greener. We won't need giant sheep, just the normal sort."

At that moment they heard a terrible sound. It was like a howl combined with a scream. It was the sound you'd expect to come from a monster.

"What on earth ..." began Tiger, the hair standing up on his neck.

"Tasmanian devil!" yelled Mrs Unwin. "But, no, surely that was too loud?"

"How big is a Tasmanian devil?" asked Tiger.

"About the size of a small dog," said Mr Unwin. "Usually ..."

All of them had the same idea. On this farm what counted as usual was very different from everywhere else.

45

Ant ran to the window. Outside he saw a sight that matched the terrifying sound they'd heard.

"It *is* a Tasmanian devil," he said in a trembling voice. "And it's as big as a rhino. AND IT'S COMING OUR WAY!"

The others joined him at the window. The creature they saw was like something out of a nightmare. It was mainly black with a few white splotches. Its legs were quite short and its body rather fat. Its head was huge and ugly and snarling, and its mouth was full of sharp white fangs.

"Quick, lock the doors and shut the windows," said Mr Unwin. "If it gets in here we're finished!"

The adults and children rushed around making sure the doors and windows were locked. Outside they heard the chilling screech of the horrible creature.

"Upstairs, everyone, and keep quiet!" whispered Mrs Unwin.

They ran up the stairs and crouched silently in one of the bedrooms. Tiger peeped over the windowsill. At exactly that moment the giant Tasmanian devil stood up on its back legs and looked in, giving Tiger the shock of his life. He staggered back from the window. Ant put his hand over his mouth to stifle the cry of fear that would otherwise have emerged.

They felt sure the devil must be able to see them and smash its way in. But after a quick snuffle it moved on.

"It must only have been able to see its reflection in the glass," said Ant.

"It's no good trying to shrink it with our watches. They won't be powerful enough, not with just the two of us," replied Ant. "We need the others. They should be back soon ... I hope."

"I've just had a thought," said Tiger. "What about the sheep? Won't the Tasmanian devil ...?"

Now they all went to the window.

Tiger was right. The huge carnivore was sniffing the air. It turned its savage head towards the barn, looked back once at the house, and then began to move towards the helpless sheep.

***

Meanwhile, the Driller burrowed on underground. Max and Cat were completely unaware of the Tasmanian terror on the surface.

"There it is!" said Max, pointing to a flashing light on the display screen. "This shouldn't take too long now."

Cat nodded and powered the Driller forwards through the dark soil.

Chapter 10 – Trapped!

"We've got to do something!" yelled Tiger, running out of the room and back down to the kitchen. Ant and the Unwins quickly followed behind him.

"Let's get its attention," said Ant.

"It's too dangerous," puffed Mrs Unwin. "We've got to look after you."

"I think we're fairly safe in the house," her husband replied. "We can hide in the basement if it tries to get in."

"We have to save the sheep." Tiger opened the window and started yelling. "Oi, stinky! Over here!"

Ant joined him at the window. He banged two saucepans together.

It worked. The giant devil turned away from the defenceless sheep, and prowled back to the house.

Back in the Driller, Cat carefully manoeuvred the Driller's powerful front paws to grab the meteorite. "Got it," she said. "Now to shrink it."

SMASH!

The Tasmanian devil shoved its snout through the kitchen window, chattering and snarling as it got a whiff of the people inside. Glass showered everywhere.

"Run!" cried Ant, and they followed Mr Unwin towards the cellar.

The devil tried to get through the window frame, but it was too fat. It moved on to the front door, bashing it down with its strong head. It caught a glimpse of the children as they headed down towards the cellar, and with a massive heave, it squeezed through. But it only managed to get half way in. And there it stayed, caught like a rat in a trap – a very big rat! It thrashed and writhed, but couldn't get in or out.

"I think its stuck," said Tiger. "Let's get out through the back door."

Out in the yard they saw a very welcome sight. Max and Cat were running towards them.

"About time!" said Tiger.

"What's going on here?" asked Max, staring in amazement at the back end of the gigantic Tasmanian devil still stuck in the doorway.

"We'll explain later," said Ant. "For now, can we shrink this guy, before he gets free and eats us and everything else on this farm?"

With the Unwins back inside the house, Team X lined up and zapped the angry Tasmanian devil. For a couple of seconds it seemed to forget that it wasn't a monster anymore and ran towards the children, still making that weird screaming growl. But now it was only the size of a piglet. Max stamped his foot and growled back, and the devil stopped dead in its tracks, turned tail and ran away, squealing.

Chapter 11 – Home again

It was time to go home.

The children had helped sort out the mess in the Unwin's farmhouse, and they had all had another slice of cake.

"I think we've all learned a valuable lesson here," said Max. "If you mess with nature, you never know what the consequences will be."

"That's very true," said Mr Unwin. "And from now on all the animals on this farm are going to be the regulation size. No more giant sheep or devils for us!"

"According to my calculations," said Ant, "the water in the lake should be back to normal in another hour – just make sure nothing else drinks from it before then."

"Fair enough," said Mr Unwin. "And you make sure you come back and see us in a year. With all that fresh water, we'll have the best farm and the best nature reserve on the whole of Tasmania."

Team X waved a last farewell and set off for the X-gate, out of sight.

Mr and Mrs Unwin took a walk out to the barn to make sure the sheep were all OK. They seemed to have recovered from the fright of the giant Tasmanian devil and were busy munching on their hay, so Mr and Mrs Unwin turned to go back to their house.

What they didn't notice was the creature with a stripy back slip out from the trees, moving with the stealth of an animal no one had seen in decades. It was bigger than the devil, and, apart from that stripy back, it looked a lot like a wolf. It had been hiding for a long, long time, and now the Tasmanian tiger was thirsty!

HIGHLY CONFIDENTIAL

From: DAY, Dani
To: STING, Charles

Subject: TEAM X MISSION UPDATE

🖇 Mission photos

Dear Charles,

I am pleased to report that Mission Tasmanian Terror was a success.

Team X discovered that the mysterious rocks and slime that were reported to have appeared in Tasmania, were connected. The rocks were discovered to be giant snails, which were creating the slime.

Team X's investigations led them to a local farm. There they found a farmer, Bill Unwin, who claimed to have witnessed a meteorite shower. The meteorite contaminated a lake on his farm. Animals that drank water from the lake were growing to unusual sizes and, in the case of the snails, exploding.

The meteorite was neutralized and all animals returned to their normal size.

Regards

Dani
Senior Scientist,
NICE

Find out more ...

For more **unexplained** adventures, read *Storm Chasers* ...

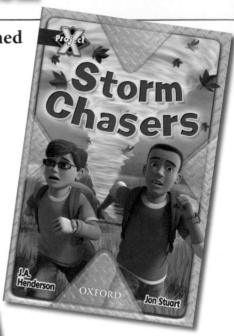

and *Ultimate Takeover*.